DRAGON

HILARY McKAY

With illustrations by

Mike Phillips

Barrington  Stoke

To Dip, with love

First published in 2017 in Great Britain by
BARRINGTON STOKE LTD
18 Walker Street, Edinburgh, EH3 7LP

This 4u2read edition based on *Dragon*
(Barrington Stoke, 2008)

Text © 2017 Hilary McKay
Illustrations © 2008 & 2017 Mike Phillips

The moral right of Hilary McKay and Mike Phillips to be
identified as the author and illustrator of this work has been
asserted in accordance with the Copyright, Designs and
Patents Act, 1988

A CIP catalogue record for this book is available
from the British Library upon request

ISBN: 978-1-78112-598-4

Printed in China by Leo

Contents

Chapter 1
Witch Towers

Max was 10 years old. He lived with his Aunt Emma.

Aunt Emma was a witch. She had a pointy hat and black clothes. She had all the witchy things that witches have. She lived in a place called Witch Towers.

She was not like any other aunt in the world.

Max and Aunt Emma liked each other, but Witch Towers was not a very peaceful place. Max was very stubborn. Aunt Emma had a temper.

A lot of the trouble at Witch Towers was because of Max's bedroom.

The mess in Max's bedroom was awful. If you opened the door, the junk came tumbling down the stairs.

This made Aunt Emma very angry. She would bang her broomstick on the floor. "I shall put up with no more!" she would shout.

Max would just shrug.

This made Aunt Emma even more cross. Sparks fell out of her witchy silver hair and flew across the floor.

"It's not that far to the edge of the world, where children aren't allowed!" she shouted.

"I have plenty of friends who live there! One day I'll go and join them! Then what will you do?"

Max didn't worry one bit. He knew Aunt Emma wouldn't go and live at the edge of the world. He knew she always calmed down in the end.

When Max was 10 he started school in the village across the fields. The village was called Sleepy Hollow.

In Sleepy Hollow no one believed in witches. Max found this out on his first day at school.

"Why didn't you come here years ago?" everyone asked.

"I didn't need to come to school," Max said. "I had my aunt to teach me things."

"Your aunt!" they said. "What did she teach you?"

"Well," said Max. "Reading and writing. A is for Abracadabra ..."

"WHAT!" everyone shouted.

"B is for Black," Max went on. "C is for Cat. D is for Dragon's eggs ..."

Everyone started laughing.

"What about P is for Pointy hats!" someone shouted. "Is your aunt some kind of witch?"

"Of course she's a witch!" Max said.

They laughed even more and they made signs to each other to show that Max was crazy. He could see they didn't believe him at all.

"My aunt lives in Witch Towers," he said. "Not that far from the edge of the world!"

"Oh yes!" Everyone laughed. "As if! Like we're going to believe that! Not!"

And then they walked off. All except one.

Timmy Green.

"I believe you," Timmy Green said. "I believe you, Max!"

From that moment Max and Timmy Green were friends.

Timmy Green did not have a mother or father. He lived in the Children's Home in the village.

Timmy and Max were not at all alike.

Max was tall. Timmy was small. Max was scared of almost nothing, but Timmy was scared of almost everything.

"I like books," Timmy told Max. "They tell you things it's good to know."

"I know everything I need to know already," Max said. "I only came to school because my aunt made me. She got in a huff after P is for Porridge and she said I could find out the rest at school."

"You can!" Timmy said. "After P, it's Q. Q is for Quiet."

"I like Noise," Max said.

"Then R," Timmy said. "R is for Rabbits."

"I know about rabbits," Max said.

"S is for School ..." Timmy went on.

Max yawned.

"T is for Timmy ..."

"I like T is for Timmy," Max said. "Stop there."

Chapter 2
Max's Great Secret

Max told Timmy about Witch Towers.

"It's over there across the fields," he said. "It has little pointed roofs and a huge wooden door. There's a big bell over the door and a rope to make it ring. And the rooms are dark with spiders everywhere."

Timmy gulped. He didn't like spiders.

"There are empty attics," Max said, "and they're haunted. I never go up there."

Timmy shivered.

"The roof is my favourite place," Max said. "There's a little flat place in the middle with

pointed roofs all around. Oh, and there's a toad garden. My aunt likes toads. Big, warty ones. I'll show you when you visit me."

Timmy shuddered.

"V ... v ... v ... visit you?" he said.

"We can climb the roof and look down over the edge," Max told him. "And you can see my witchy aunt when she has a huff. When can you come? Today?"

"N ... n ... not today," said Timmy.

"Tomorrow?" said Max.

"No," said Timmy. "N ... n ... not tomorrow."

"Soon?"

"M ... m ... maybe."

"Good," said Max. "Then I'll show you my Great Secret that I found in the fields. I've

been dying to show someone. It's hidden under my bed. Guess what it is! I'll give you a clue, it's gold! And it's warm. Very, very heavy and bigger than a football. But it's egg-shaped, of course!"

"Is it an egg?" Timmy asked.

"You guessed that fast!" Max said. "But what sort of egg? You'll never guess! My aunt has always wanted one, that's why I've got to keep it such a secret!"

Timmy was staring at Max with his eyes wide open.

Timmy had read every single book in the library. He had read all the Nature books twice. He knew which eggs were gold and heavy and bigger than a football.

He said, "It's a dra ... dra ... a dragon's egg!"

"Yes," Max said. "Clever T for Timmy!"

"B ... b ... but dragons' eggs are very dangerous!" Timmy said. "I read it in a book ..."

"You can't believe books!" said Max. "They're not real life! Now, I know ALL about dragons' eggs! I've GOT a dragon's egg! I'm going to keep it until it hatches and then I'll have a baby dragon!"

"But what will you do with a baby dragon?" Timmy asked.

"I shall keep it on the roof!" said Max.

"It will escape," said Timmy.

"I will tame it," said Max.

"It will grow very big."

"The roof is huge."

"What about when it learns to fly?"

"It hasn't even hatched yet," said Max.

Chapter 3
Aunt Emma's Huff

Max made a new notice for his bedroom door. The notice was to keep his aunt out. That way, she wouldn't find the dragon's egg.

The notice said –

> KNOCK AND KNOCK AND KNOCK
> BUT DON'T COME IN!
>
> MAX'S ROOM, PRIVATE PLACE,
> DO NOT DARE SHOW YOUR FACE.

The notice worked. It kept Aunt Emma out. But it made her very cross. She banged the floor with her broomstick and sparks flew out of her hair and she said she would go to the edge of the world where no children were allowed.

Then Max made a new notice. It said –

NO FREAKY BROOMSTICK PEOPLE

When Aunt Emma saw the notice she was so cross that she pulled open Max's door to tell him off.

A wave of old clothes, footballs, dirty plates, muddy boots, and a hundred other things fell out of the door and rolled Aunt Emma down the stairs and into the garden.

Then Aunt Emma had her biggest huff ever.

Sparks shot out of her hair like comets.

She grabbed her broomstick and there was a white flash of fire.

"I'm off!" Aunt Emma said. "To the edge of the world! And I won't be back until you have tidied your bedroom!"

Then there was a bang and a roar like thunder and a lot of black smoke.

After that there was nothing.

No broomstick. No pointy hat. No Aunt Emma.

Max stood in the garden. It smelled like fireworks.

The silence was awful.

Then from up in his bedroom he heard a little sound. A clink like breaking china.

Perhaps it was because of the enormous bang. Perhaps it would have happened anyway.

The dragon's egg was hatching.

Chapter 4
All Alone

Max ran up to his room as fast as he could. He was sure a baby dragon would be waiting there.

But nothing had changed. He pulled the dragon's egg out from under his bed, and it was as gold and solid as ever.

Then Max spotted something new.

There was a dark zig-zag line across the gold shell.

Max wished that Timmy could see the egg hatching too.

Over in the village, everyone had noticed the flash of white light, the thick black smoke and the rumble of the broomstick.

"Lightning!" they said. "Lightning has hit poor Miss Emma's house!"

In no time at all about a hundred people were running to the rescue. They took first aid boxes, sandwiches, blankets and cameras. They ordered the children to stay behind. The children didn't listen.

But when they all got to Witch Towers they were sorry to see that it looked just the same as always.

No one came when they banged on the door.

Max was still in his room.

He heard the bangs, but he said, "I can't answer the door! The egg could hatch at any moment! Whoever it is will have to go away."

But no one went away. Instead Max heard footsteps and helpful voices on the stairs.

"Cooee! Anyone home, Miss Emma?"

"We thought we should pop over!"

"Max? Are you there, Max, dear?"

"Bother!" said Max.

The footsteps stopped at his bedroom door. He heard whispering. People were reading his notice.

"Bother, oh bother, oh BOTHER!" Max grumbled. He opened his bedroom door, stepped outside and closed it again.

There was a huge crowd on the landing and on the stairs.

"There's loads of you!" Max said. "Did Timmy come?"

The crowd looked at each other, and then shook their heads.

"Pity," Max said. "I'm afraid I'm busy! So, goodbye."

No one took this big hint. They all began to talk at once.

"Thank goodness you're not hurt!"

"What a very rude notice on your door, Max!"

"Your poor dear aunt! Where is she?"

"Gone," Max said. All he wanted was to get back to his dragon's egg.

"Gone?" someone asked.

"On her broomstick," Max said. "That was the bang you heard. It wasn't lightning at all!"

But no one was listening. "Struck by lightning!" they said. "How very sad! She must have been vaporised!"

"Vaporised?" Max said.

"Frizzled into nothing, dear," the lady from the Children's Home said. "You must come back with us! We are very crowded, but after your sad loss …"

"You don't understand!" Max said. "She wasn't frizzled! There was no lightning! She just whizzed off on her broomstick in a huff. And I can't come with you, I'm very busy here!"

No one believed Max. They said he was unkind. They said he wasn't funny. They said what a dreadful way to talk about his poor frizzled aunt.

They wouldn't listen when Max said he'd be all right on his own.

"What if you need help?" they said. "No one will know."

"I'll shout!" Max said. "I'll yell! I'll ring the bell!"

Max pushed past all the people and ran downstairs. He pulled a table onto the front porch, lifted a chair onto the table, stood on the chair and pulled the long bell rope.

The noise made everyone jam their hands on their ears.

"You'd hear that!" Max said.

Even so, it was a long time before they agreed that Max could stay at Witch Towers just for one more night. They made him say that he would ring the bell the moment he needed them, and they promised they would come running the moment they heard it.

After that they left the sandwiches they had brought in tidy heaps around the garden.

Then they went home.

Max had been worrying about his dragon's egg all the time. He rushed back to it as soon as the crowd had gone.

It was just as he had left it, warm and round, with a dark zig-zag line across the gold shell.

"Good," Max said, and he sat down on the floor by the egg. He tried to feel happy that he

hadn't missed anything, and that his aunt had gone, and that the crowd had gone. Now he was free to do just as he liked.

"Perfect," Max said. "Perfect, but a bit lonely."

He wished that Timmy was there.

Chapter 5
The Bell

The house was quiet. There was no witchy singing downstairs. No rattle of witchy cooking from the kitchen. No one in the garden, looking after the toads.

"Everyone said they would come if I rang the bell," Max told his dragon's egg.

It lay as silent as a stone.

"I bet they wouldn't come," Max said. "Maybe they wouldn't even hear it."

In the end Max made up his mind to ring the bell to find out. He rang and rang it.

It boomed over the fields to the village, where the last of the crowd had just arrived home. They heard it, and they remembered their promise. They turned and rushed back the way they had come.

Max was so glad to see them that he made a small speech.

"Thank you," he said. "I was just testing to make sure you could hear it."

The crowd clapped. They were pleased to be thanked. They said it was a good idea to test the bell. Then they said goodbye, and went home.

Max went to see if his dragon's egg had hatched, and it hadn't.

"They all came!" Max said to the egg. "Everyone! Well, everyone but Timmy. He was probably reading and didn't hear. Sometimes he doesn't. I've noticed that."

The silence was awful.

"I bet no one would come if I rang that bell again!" Max said. "They'd say, 'It's just a test,' and stay where they were!"

Max was wrong. They did come. Not as many this time, but still a crowd.

Max made another speech.

"I didn't think you'd come back again!" he said. "That's why I rang the bell! But you did. So thank you. Again."

No one clapped. They went home and they didn't wave goodbye.

"Timmy didn't come," Max said, when he was back upstairs with his dragon's egg. "He must still be reading." Then he thought about the people. "They were cross," he told the dragon's egg. "I should have said, 'Sorry', but I forgot. I'll ring the bell and say it now." So he did.

The people who came back looked very tired and very grumpy. They said, "We suppose you think this is funny! But we don't."

And then they went away.

Max went back up to his bedroom and he was so bored he almost thought to tidy it up.

"I'm in trouble now," he told the egg. "No one's going to come. Not even if I ring the bell till it cracks! I could be in terrible danger and no one would come ..."

This was such a sad idea that Max could hardly bear it. He was sad as he went downstairs. He was sad as he rang the bell. He knew no help would ever arrive.

Three people came.

Max was so happy to see them that he laughed out loud. No one else laughed.

One of them was the lady from the Children's Home.

"Max," she said. "Go and get your things!
We're taking you back with us. You can share
Timmy's room."

For a moment Max thought that was a good idea. Then he thought of his dragon's egg. He couldn't take it with him.

It was much too heavy to carry so far. Anyway, no pets were allowed at the Children's Home. Not even rabbits. Most of all not baby dragons.

So Max did the only thing he could think of. He dashed inside and slammed the door. He thought they might come after him, but they didn't. He watched from the window as they trailed back across the fields.

They looked so tired that he wanted to ring the bell and bring them back to say, "I'm sorry if you're tired because of me."

But he didn't.

All this time, Timmy Green had been reading in his little bedroom in the Children's Home.

Timmy was scared.

Every time the bell had rung Timmy was more scared. He thought of toads and spiders and haunted attics. He thought about the dragon's egg that Max kept under his bed. And how Max didn't know how dangerous the egg was. But when the bell rang he couldn't make himself rush across the fields.

"There are plenty of people without me," he said to himself each time the bell rang, but he didn't feel good.

"I'm a coward," he told himself, "and I don't deserve a brave friend like Max."

Chapter 6
Dragon!

While Timmy was thinking about Max, Max was plodding up to his bedroom and thinking about Timmy.

"What was it that Timmy wanted to tell me about dragons' eggs?" he said. "He said they were dangerous! How can an egg be dangerous?"

Max knew that dragons were quite safe. He had asked Aunt Emma about them, soon after he found the egg.

"Dragons?" she had said. "Dangerous? Not if you know how to handle them! Messy? Yes. Dangerous? No. Rather like children."

Max opened his door. The dragon's egg was still there, just as he had left it.

"Doesn't look dangerous to me!" he said.

BANG!!!

Max fell over so hard his head cracked off the wall. There was a smell like a million hard-boiled eggs. Chunks of shell as sharp and thick as broken flowerpots whizzed past his eyes. They hit the walls and made dust fall in showers like dirty snow.

One bit of shell thumped into the wooden door just behind Max and stuck there like a knife.

At last Max knew what Timmy had been trying to tell him about dragons' eggs.

Dragons' eggs didn't hatch. Dragons' eggs exploded!

"Gosh!" Max groaned. "I see why Timmy said they were dangerous!"

Max rubbed the dust from his eyes and remembered his problems had only just begun. There should be a dragon! Where was it?

It was curled under his table, in the middle of a thick green puddle. It was all sticky with a sort of eggy goo. It smelled awful.

Max held out his hand and the dragon hissed and snarled. The green puddle got bigger.

Aunt Emma knew about dragons. She would have said, "What a beauty!" She would have seen the green and golden scales, the ruby eyes, and the red bumps that would one day be wings.

But to Max it looked like a monster. And it smelled like a monster. And it ate like a monster.

First it ate a sock. Then it spotted a pair of toads that had followed Max upstairs from the garden.

"Stop!" Max shouted. He jumped to try and save the toads, slipped in the green goo and cut his hand on a bit of shell.

The dragon gobbled up the toads, slid towards Max and licked the blood on his hand. Then it tried to eat a model of a Viking ship from under Max's table.

The sharp wooden mast of the ship got stuck in the dragon's throat. The dragon croaked and choked and hissed. Max ran after it. He thumped the dragon's back until at last the ship came up again, along with the sock and the toads, all of them in bits and pieces.

"I'm taking you outside!" Max told the
dragon as it made another green puddle on
the floor. "Not into the garden, you'll eat
the toads. It will have to be the roof. I know
Timmy said not to keep dragons on the roof,
but I don't care!"

It wasn't easy to get the dragon on the roof.
Max put a belt round its neck and tied some
socks together to make a lead to pull it along.

Out in the open air the baby dragon became quieter. But it licked the blood from Max's cut hand in such a hungry way that Max began to worry. He tied it to a drainpipe, and thought about what he could feed it.

"Sandwiches!" he remembered. "There are loads of sandwiches in the garden."

Max pushed open the front door, and stepped out into the garden to collect the sandwiches. It was nice to breathe the fresh air outside. He looked towards the village, where one light was shining. He looked up at the sky and saw the first star.

Chapter 7
Max in Trouble

The long summer day was coming to an end. Aunt Emma always made Max wish on the first star in the night sky. She had told him the spell –

"*Star light, star bright, first star I see tonight, I wish I may, I wish I might, have the wish I wish tonight.*"

"I wish Aunt Emma would come back," Max said in a tired voice. "I wish Timmy was here. I wish the dragon would be good. I wish everything would be all right in the morning."

More stars were coming out all the time.

They shone like tiny sparks of silver. The pointed roofs looked sharp and black against the evening sky.

Just then Max heard something. A scrabbling sound, high up on the roof.

The sound grew louder. A head with two ruby eyes rose up, dark against the stars.

There was the screech of claws on tiles. There was a yowl of fear.

Something slid down the roof and landed at Max's feet. It was the lead Max had made of socks.

Timmy had been right again.

You couldn't keep a dragon on a roof.

Max's dragon was half way over the top already.

"Don't move till I get there!" Max yelled. He flung down the sandwiches and ran. The bell rope tripped him up as he rushed past. DONG went the bell.

Max didn't even notice.

He ran up all the stairs to the top of the house, out onto the roof, across the flat place in the middle, and up the slope to the highest point.

He was just in time to catch the dragon's tail as it tumbled over the edge.

In the village everyone had gone to bed cross and early. Timmy was the only person who heard the bell ring. He put down his book

and tip-toed outside. It was dark, and very still.

Bang, bang, bang went Timmy's heart, as he thought of toads and witches and ghosts and dragons.

He didn't know what to do.

"If it rings again," he said at last, "I will wake someone up."

But it didn't ring again. No one woke up. There was just Timmy, alone in the street. It was so quiet he began to hope he had dreamed the ringing of the bell.

But he knew that was not true and so he set off down the road.

"I had better be brave," Timmy said to Timmy. "Because there is only me."

Chapter 8
Timmy to the Rescue

Up on the roof Max and the dragon were not having a good time. The dragon and the top half of Max hung down on one side of the pointed roof. The bottom half of Max hung down the other.

They were not very well balanced.

Sometimes Max pulled the dragon a little bit backwards. Sometimes the dragon slipped and pulled them both a little bit forwards.

Those were the worst times.

Max had two choices. He could let go, or he could hold on.

He held on.

After a while the dragon went to sleep, upside down, like a bat. Max grew very cold and very, very bored.

"How odd," Max said out loud, to make the night seem less lonely. "How odd to be bored when you're hanging upside down in the dark, holding a dragon by the tail! And all alone because your aunt the witch has vanished on her broomstick with a flash and a bang! How can all that be boring?"

"I don't know," Max said to Max, "but it is."

All this time, Timmy was having a horrible walk. Every minute it had grown darker, every minute he had grown more scared.

Now at last he was at Max's garden gate.

The first Max knew of this was an odd singing from far below him.

"Toads, toads, move out of the way!" the singing went. "Because I can't see where you are in the dark! Toads, toads ..."

Timmy was making his way to the front door, and he was terribly afraid he'd step on a toad.

A minute later he knocked.

Next, he pushed the door open, and called out in a scared voice into the dark rooms, "Max! Max!" Then he climbed the stairs.

Timmy found the two rooms at the top of the stairs. First he found Aunt Emma's room, as tidy as a picture in a book. Then he found the wild mess of a room that was where Max lived. He saw that the dragon's egg had hatched and it made his heart thump harder than ever.

He wanted to run away, but he didn't.

Instead he climbed the next lot of stairs. He passed the attics that Max said were haunted. He came out onto the high flat place on the roof.

It was so dark that at first Timmy couldn't see Max, but then he heard a squeaky voice say, "Help, help!" in an uncomfy upside-down way.

"Where are you?" Timmy shouted, but then he saw the bottom half of Max hung over the peak of the roof. Timmy guessed the top half was not far away.

A moment later Timmy was scrabbling up the tiles to get hold of Max's legs. When he had got them, he pulled as hard as he could. Very soon after that, Max toppled down on top of him. The baby dragon (still fast asleep) toppled down behind, and squashed them both.

"Thanks, Timmy," Max said. "I was getting really bored."

Chapter 9
The Tidy Up

Now Max and Timmy had to decide what to do with the dragon. It was still asleep, so the easiest thing was to put it to bed.

"But not in my room!" Max said.

So he and Timmy put the baby dragon to sleep in Aunt Emma's bed. It looked very comfy, tucked up under her black quilt.

"It's a very rare sort of dragon," Timmy whispered. "It may be the only one in the country."

"Good!" Max said. "One dragon like this is plenty! Have you seen what it's done to my bedroom? I don't think I'll ever be able to tidy it up."

But they did tidy Max's bedroom. They flung the chunks of gold shell out of the window, mopped up the green puddles and swept away the dust. They rammed everything into drawers and cupboards and rubbish bins – all the clothes, bits of paper, apple cores, sticks, half-finished models, pencils, chalks, odd-shaped stones, empty mugs, tangled kites, dirty bottles and boots and shoes. All the things Max had collected over the last 10 years.

It took them until 2 a.m.

Then Max and Timmy took the blankets and pillows up onto the roof and made their beds there. They couldn't sleep in Max's room because it still smelled of hatching dragon. But it was tidy at last.

"Aunt Emma will be glad when she comes back and sees it," Max said.

"Oh, Max," Timmy said, "I'm afraid people who have been struck by lightning don't come back."

"She wasn't struck by lightning," Max said with a yawn. "She went off on her broomstick to visit her friends at the edge of the world. She said she'd come back when I tidied my room. And I have," he said, and he fell asleep.

Chapter 10
Coming Home

When Max and Timmy woke up, bright sunshine was shining down on their faces.

They could hear a witchy voice.

"Down!" the voice ordered. "Sit! Good boy! Now, come!"

"She's back!" Max shouted. He had missed his aunt very much. He and Timmy flung off their blankets and rushed to look down into the garden.

Black sheets and pillowcases were flapping on the washing line. Aunt Emma and the small golden dragon were on the grass.

"Stay!" Aunt Emma ordered, and the dragon stayed as still as a stone.

"It's a very rare one!" Timmy shouted. "I've seen them in a book!"

"I've wanted one for years," Aunt Emma shouted back. "Hello, Max!"

"Hello!" Max called, as happy as anything.

"I'm very glad to see you have tidied your room, but next time a baby dragon hatches and you boys put in my bed, please wash it first! And why are there sandwiches all over the garden?"

"They came from the village," Max told her. "They brought them for me because they thought you'd been struck by lightning."

"Struck by lightning?" Aunt Emma said.

"They don't believe you're a witch," Max said. "No one does, do they, Timmy?"

"They think you're a nice old lady," said Timmy. "They don't think you're a witch, because you don't do spells."

"I do them all the time," said Aunt Emma. She looked a bit cross as she fed the dragon a sandwich.

"I did a spell last night," Max told her. "The star one."

"Did it work?" Aunt Emma asked.

Max thought about his wishes. "Yes," he said. "It did."

That morning was the start of lots of good times. Max and Aunt Emma made friends again. The dragon grew more and more beautiful. Timmy came to Witch Towers for the longest sleepover ever. It lasted until he grew up.

Every day Timmy and Max walked across the fields to Sleepy Hollow School.

And one day the dragon went too. He tracked Max and Timmy all the way from Witch Towers.

The dragon was much bigger now. He was learning to fly, and he could already blow smoke that was almost hot.

Behind the dragon came Aunt Emma with her broomstick. Sparks flew out of her hair as she rushed to catch him.

"Stamp those sparks out!" Timmy shouted to the rest of the school, as he and Max ran to help her. "Quick, or they'll scorch the grass!"

But no one came to help. They all ran inside. Only when Aunt Emma had swept the dragon out of the playground with her broomstick did some of the children and teachers come out. Then everyone stamped on the grass in a nervous way and said, "It's all right for you two! You're not scared because you're used to dragons and witches!"

This made Max and Timmy laugh very much.

"How do you know she's not just a nice old lady?" asked Max.

"Like we're going to believe that!" everyone said. "Not!"

And when Max and Timmy heard this they laughed and laughed. They nearly fell over, laughing.